25 JUL 2022

5 SEP 2022

Books should be returned or renewed by the last date above. Renew by phone **03000 41 31 31** or online *www.kent.gov.uk/libs*

FOOTBALL
MAD

Teamwork!

PAUL STEWART

Illustrated by
Michael Broad

Barrington Stoke

First published in 2022 in Great Britain by
Barrington Stoke Ltd
18 Walker Street, Edinburgh, EH3 7LP

www.barringtonstoke.co.uk

This story was first published in a different form
as *Football Mad 4: Teamwork!* (Scholastic, 2000)

Text © 2022 Paul Stewart
Illustrations © 2022 Michael Broad

A CIP catalogue record for this book is available
from the British Library upon request

ISBN: 978-1-78112-936-4

Printed by Hussar Books, Poland

For Jose and Anna

Chapter 1

"I know that," said Scott hotly. "It's just ..."
He shook his head. Everything that Danny and
Jack said made sense, but it didn't make Scott
feel any better.

The three friends were up the rec having
a breather in the middle of a long game of
three-'n'-in. Danny and Jack were lying on the
grass. Scott was stomping about trying to work
things out in his head.

"It's just not right," he said. "Albion spotted
him first. They taught him everything he
knows! And now United's poached him."

"Would you turn down an offer of fifty million?" Jack asked.

Scott frowned. "Yes," he said. "Yes, I would."

Jack snorted. "As if!"

"I *would*!" Scott shouted. "I don't know how Liam Griggs can live with himself."

The evening before, the two clubs had met up for the first time since Liam Griggs had moved from Albion to United – and Griggs had scored a goal against his old team. Scott could not believe it. And one day on, he was still angry.

"After everything Albion did for him," he said. "He's a traitor!"

"What did you expect him to do?" Jack asked. "He plays for United now. Of course he's gonna try and score for them," he said. "It's the team that's important, not the individual player."

"I *know* that!" said Scott. "But I still think—"

"Oh, Scott!" said Danny. "Give it a rest, will you?"

Scott fell silent and walked away. He knew he was going on a bit – but then he was a true Albion supporter. He'd stuck with them through thick and thin. Danny and Jack didn't care as much. What Liam Griggs had done was no big deal to them.

*

Liam Griggs!

For as far back as Scott could remember, Liam Griggs had been his hero. A talented local lad, Griggs was spotted by a football scout and made it big playing for Albion. Scott had saved up for a replica shirt with Griggs' name and number on the back. He had a match ticket, signed by Griggs. And a huge poster of him on his wall ...

But now, all of those things were in a box under Scott's bed. He would take them out again when Liam Griggs did the right thing and came back to Albion. Where he belonged!

Scott had often dreamed that an Albion scout would spot *him*. That they would see *his* talent. That they would offer *him* the chance to play for the team. *He* wouldn't let them down. *He* would stay loyal ...

Chapter 2

Assembly was not the kids' favourite part of the day, but that Wednesday morning, Mrs Brown, their headteacher, had something important to say. Something which made everyone in Year 7 sit up and listen.

"First of all, I want to congratulate all of you who took part in the Easter Fair," she said. "Especially the Under-12 football team ..."

Everyone smiled and nodded. Scott, Danny and Jack looked at each other proudly.

"As I'm sure you all know, Dale beat Barfield, 2–1, in the final of the Langton Town Junior Cup."

A cheer went up.

"What you may not know," Mrs Brown went on, "is that the crowds that went to the match all visited the Easter Fair too, so we had a fantastic day. I'm pleased to announce that the amount of money everyone raised was an incredible ..."

A hush fell. You could have heard a pin drop. The money was all going to a new children's ward at the local hospital. So how much money was it?

"Five thousand, seven hundred and forty-six pounds. And twenty-seven pence."

There was a gasp, followed by a moment of silence – and then an enormous roar. Mrs Brown waited for the clapping and cheering to finish before she spoke again.

"The money will all go to the hospital fund," she said. "And they are very grateful. But ..."

She looked around at the faces of the boys and girls in the hall. "Even after all the money you raised at the Easter Fair, the hospital still needs a lot more before they can start work on the new children's ward. So I want you all to put on your thinking caps and come up with ideas for raising more money. Bring-and-buy sales. Sponsored walks. Raffles. Christmas cards."

"What about a non-uniform day?" Max Novak called out. "Everyone pays two pounds to wear what they want."

"Excellent idea, Max," said Mrs Brown. "I—"

"Or a marathon read-in," suggested Jemima Blake, who was a bit of a geek.

"Or a disco," shouted Tanya Smith, who wasn't.

Mrs Brown called for quiet. "If anyone has a good idea, please talk about it to your form teacher." She smiled. "And good luck, all of you."

As the boys and girls headed for their lessons, everyone was talking about the assembly. Scott, Danny and Jack had English first lesson with Miss Turner – who was also their form-teacher. The moment they walked into the classroom, all three cornered her.

"Miss, Miss, Miss," they all went.

"We've had a brilliant idea," said Scott.

"For raising money," Danny explained.

Scott grinned. "A charity football match," he said.

Miss Turner smiled. "Really?"  she said. "Sometimes I think the world's gone football mad."

"But, Miss," said Jack. "Mrs Brown said that people spent lots of money at the Easter Fair because of the football. So why don't we have another match?"

"But this time, everyone has to pay to watch it," said Scott.

Miss Turner nodded. "And who would you play?" she asked.

Scott looked down. "We thought we could play against the teachers," he said with a little smile.

"You could play in goal, Miss," said Danny.

"Yes, nice idea," said Miss Turner. "But I don't think so." She frowned. "What about one of the other local schools? Or perhaps a fathers' – a *parents'* – team?"

Scott nodded. "We could do," he said, "but—"

"I've got a much better idea," someone called out from the back of the class.

Everyone turned and looked at Ruby Taylor.

"Well?" said Miss Turner.

Ruby grinned. "Simple," she said. "We make it girls against boys."

For a moment, no one said a thing. They were all thinking about what Ruby had said. Girls against boys. It would be a walkover – and who'd want to pay to watch a match like that? Then again, the girls' team really wasn't bad. They'd made it to the semis of the local Girls' Club League. And Ruby herself was a very determined – and talented – captain.

A low mutter went round the classroom. It grew louder and louder, until everyone was chanting.

"Boys! Boys! Boys!" cried the boys.

"Girls! Girls! Girls!" the girls shouted back.

Miss Turner's arm shot up. She wanted quiet and she wanted it now.

"Girls!" one voice shouted. It was Ruby's best friend, Tanya. She spun round. "Whoops! Sorry, Miss."

"*Humph*," said Miss Turner. She looked around at the sea of faces. "Well," she said at last, "if there's as much interest in the match *outside* the class as there is *inside*, you could do very well indeed." She smiled. "I'll talk to Mrs Brown at break."

Chapter 3

Mrs Brown thought that the football competition was a fantastic idea, and the match was fixed for Wednesday, 1 May. That gave both teams two weeks to practise – and everyone else time to organise the event. And as the days passed and the match got nearer, the boys and girls of Dale Juniors grew more and more excited.

"So, what do you reckon the score's going to be?" Danny asked after their final Friday training session.

"3–0," said Jack.

"5–0," said Scott.

"10–0," shouted Max Novak, and a cheer went round the changing room.

Mr Berryman, the boys' football coach, laughed. "Watch out," he warned them. "From what Mrs Hopkins says, the girls' team is looking pretty sharp."

"But, sir," Danny groaned. "You don't think they could beat us, do you?"

Mr Berryman shrugged. "All I'm saying is, the match could be closer than you think."

*

The next afternoon, Scott, Danny and Jack were at the rec again.

"Do you think Mr Berryman was serious?" said Danny. "*Could* the girls beat us?"

Jack laughed. "You know how much Ruby likes winning!" he said. "What do you think, Scott?"

Scott looked up. "What was that?" he said.

"Weren't you listening?" said Jack.

"Listening?" said Scott.

"Oh, blimey!" said Danny. "You're not still thinking about Liam Griggs, are you?"

"No. Yeah. I mean ..."

"You *were*!" said Danny. He rolled his eyes. "I don't believe it!"

"It's not what you think," said Scott, and he went on to explain why Liam Griggs was on his mind again.

The day before, he'd heard Mrs Brown and Mrs Hopkins talking about who should present the trophy to the winning team. Someone famous. Someone local. Someone to do with football ...

"What about Liam Griggs?" Scott had heard Mrs Hopkins say.

Liam Griggs. The traitor. Scott had turned and walked away. He didn't want to hear Mrs Brown's reply. And anyway, these days Liam Griggs was way too big and famous to present a trophy to a bunch of schoolkids ...

*

The day of the big match came closer. The children had sold so many tickets that the school football ground just wasn't big enough. And so the two Dale Under-12s football teams – boys and girls – were going to play at the town's main sports centre.

The last time the boys played there, they had beaten Barfield Comp in the final of the Langton Town Junior Cup. It had been an important match. They'd won the hat-trick – and had the cup to prove it.

This time there was much more to lose!

"You do know that if the girls beat us, everyone is going to laugh at us," said Jack one day after school.

"They're not going to beat us," said Scott and Danny together.

Jack shrugged. "I caught the girls training yesterday," he said. "At Regan's Park. They're there every evening."

"And?" said Scott.

"They looked good," he said. "Solid. Together. They really want to win, you know."

"I'm sure they do," said Danny. "Thing is, we're not going to let them. Are we?"

"What's the matter, Jack?" Scott asked. He grinned. "Are you worried?"

Danny sniggered.

"Course not," said Jack. "But if they play like that on the day, there's no way we'll win 10–0!"

Chapter 4

The big day arrived at last. At quarter to three, the two teams were in their changing rooms getting ready.

Danny's fingers trembled as he pulled on his boots. He couldn't get the laces tied. "I'm really nervous," he whispered to Scott.

"Me too, mate," Scott admitted. They could hear the crowd outside chanting. "There's a lot of people out there."

"I know," said Danny. "But it's not that. It's—"

"It's because of who we're playing," Jack butted in.

"What, the girls' team?" said Scott. He snorted. "They can't be *that* good. Our last match against Barfield was much harder. This is going to be a piece of cake."

"But that's just it," said Jack. "Everyone's expecting us to win. All the pressure's on us."

"Jack's right," said Danny. "That's just how I feel. Under pressure. The girls have got nothing to lose. But we've got to prove ourselves."

"Yeah, well," said Scott, checking the time. "That's what we're going to do. Prove ourselves. Come on, you lot," he called out to the rest of the team. "Let's get out there."

"That's the spirit," said Mr Berryman. "And remember, this is a charity match. A bit of a laugh. So have fun!"

Up and ready, the team was just about to go out onto the pitch when there was a knock at the door. Mr Berryman opened it.

Mrs Hopkins and Ruby Taylor were standing there. Both of them looked unhappy.

"Bit of a crisis, I'm afraid," Mrs Hopkins said. "As captain, Ruby's come along with me to ask for your help. We're down to ten players. Sam broke her arm yesterday evening—"

"Falling off her stupid skateboard," said Ruby with a scowl.

"Can't you put in one of the subs?" asked Mr Berryman.

"We don't have any subs," said Mrs Hopkins. "I've just had to send Amber and Jade home. Both of them were too ill to play." She frowned. "I don't know what to do."

Outside, the people waiting to watch the match began to chant more loudly.

Mrs Hopkins turned to Mr Berryman. "We can't let all these people down."

"Of course we can't," said Mr Berryman. He rubbed his chin slowly before he replied. "It seems to me that we have two choices. Either we play ten-a-side or—"

"But, *sir!*" the boys groaned.

"It wouldn't be a proper game," said Ruby.

"And anyway, which of the boys would get dropped?" said Scott. "We *all* want to play and—"

"*Or*," Mr Berryman repeated, "one of the boys goes to play on the girls' team."

No one said a word.

"Are you sure there isn't someone else who can play?" Danny asked Ruby. "What about Ella? She used to be on your team."

"Not any more," said Ruby.

"She might chip her black nail-varnish," said Max with a laugh.

Ruby shrugged. "I hate to admit this, but ... well, there just aren't as many girls who like playing football as boys. Worse luck!"

Mr Berryman turned to the boys and put his hands on his hips. "What's it to be, then? I agree with you lot. Ten-a-side would be a bit of a let-down. The question is, who wants to play on the girls' side?"

All thirteen boys looked down at the floor.

Mrs Hopkins sighed. "Is no one going to volunteer?" she asked.

23

The boys kept their heads down.

"Then there's nothing else for it," she said. "We'll have to pick a number from a hat."

A sigh of relief went round. Everyone was safe – for the moment. And the chances of being picked were very small ...

"Just don't let it be me," they muttered to themselves as Mr Berryman wrote numbers on slips of paper – one to thirteen – folded them and dropped them into the baseball cap that Mrs Hopkins was holding.

As he finished the last number, Mr Berryman looked around. "Now, we all agree that this is the way we want to go forward, yes?"

The boys said nothing.

"*Yes?*" said Mr Berryman. "The boy who's chosen mustn't try and get out of it. There's no turning back. Do you all understand that?"

The boys looked at their boots. All they wanted now was for Mr Berryman to get on with it. Thirteen to one were pretty good odds. And yet ...

Mr Berryman put his hand into the cap and swilled it around. He pulled out one of the bits of paper. Then slowly – horribly slowly – he unfolded it. He looked at the number.

What was it? Who was going to have to play on the girls' team?

Without saying a word, Mr Berryman held the paper up. Twelve boys breathed out slowly. It wasn't them. Only one boy looked shocked. Only one ...

"But I'm captain," said Scott. "I can't—"

"Scott," said Mr Berryman. "We all agreed."

Scott gulped and turned away. He knew better than to argue. After all, he'd promised that he wouldn't. But playing for the girls! Would he ever live it down?

Mr Berryman patted him on the back.

"Well done, Scott," he said, and handed him a white top to change into. "I'm proud of you."

Mr Berryman wasn't the only one who was happy with the way things had turned out. Ruby was grinning from ear to ear. They'd bagged themselves the boys' best player.

As Scott got closer, she stepped forward and shook his hand.

"Welcome to the team," she said. "I just hope you play as well for us as you do for the boys," she added in a whisper.

Scott nodded but said nothing. It had all come as such a shock. His head was spinning, his legs were shaking – he felt sick. He was so nervous, he didn't know if he could play at all, let alone play well.

Chapter 5

A roar went up as the two teams trotted out onto the pitch. Scott heard his own name coming out of the loudspeakers as Mrs Brown announced that he'd had to change teams, and why.

As the news sank in, the crowd showed their feelings. Most of them cheered. A few laughed. And some – boys mainly – jeered the lad who was playing for the other team.

The girls' team.

Scott went bright red. This was just what he'd feared. Why couldn't they have played ten-a-side? Why had Mr Berryman picked his number? But it was all too late now. There was no turning back.

Then again, Scott thought, *just because I'm on the girls' team doesn't mean I have to help them win!*

After all, he was captain of the *boys'* team. How could he play to make them lose?

The two sides took up their positions. The crowd fell still. The referee blew his whistle. Luke chipped the ball to Jack.

The match had begun.

*

"Square ball!" Ruby yelled as Scott dribbled up the right wing.

Scott looked round. Ruby was in a good position – worse luck! If his pass was good too, she might even score.

He gave the ball a sloppy kick. It was a hopeless lay-off. Not only did it miss Ruby by a mile, but it landed straight at Wesley Hunter's feet.

Wesley didn't miss his chance. He tapped the ball past Georgia, who was racing up to tackle him, and sprinted away. Luke Edwards was making a run up the left wing. As Sarah and Eve – the girls' numbers 2 and 5 – raced towards him, Wesley dummied to the right, then punted the ball up the field.

Luke was on it like a shot. But the girls' defence was rock solid. There was no way through.

"LUKE! LUKE!" Max Novak bellowed. He was standing just outside the penalty box. Unmarked.

Luke kicked the ball across to him. The pass was high, floating – and deadly accurate. As it came down, Max took it on the volley and powered it at the goal.

Tanya dived. But she never stood a chance. The ball whistled past her fingertips and slammed into the back of the net.

A roar went up from the crowd. It was 1–0. Only twelve minutes into the match and the boys had already gone into the lead.

Ruby was so angry. "That was your fault!" she shouted at Scott as she stormed across the pitch towards him.

"*My* fault?" said Scott. "It's not my fault your defence is so rubbish."

"You set up the whole goal," Ruby yelled. "You gave them the ball!"

"Leave it out," said Scott, and turned away.

But Ruby was right – and Scott knew that he would have reacted the same way if it was his team. The trouble was, he just couldn't commit. If he did, his own team – his *real* team – might lose.

"*This* is your team now," said Ruby, as if she was reading his mind.

Scott turned and looked at her.

"The reds are the opposition," she said slowly. "You're playing for the whites. And we're 1–0 down. Keep playing the way you are and we – and that includes *you* – are going to lose." She looked hard at Scott. "Is that really what you want?"

No, Scott thought as he trotted up for the kick-off. *That's not what I want.*

Scott had never in his life played to lose.

"I'll play better," he told himself. "I'll make chances. I'll set up moves ... But I won't score. That'd be going *too* far."

As the match started up again, Scott's game did improve. His passing became more accurate; his headers more punishing; his tackles harder. The crowd saw the change in his game. The girls cheered and waved their white scarves every time he got near the opposition goal. The boys booed and whistled and jeered.

"You should have worn a skirt!" someone shouted out.

On the pitch, too, the boys were getting angry. They gave Scott dirty looks. They made nasty comments as they ran past him. But Scott didn't care. He knew now that he could never, *ever* play to lose, so he ignored them.

"Over here!" he yelled to Sarah, who was about to take a throw-in.

She twisted round and threw the ball. Scott dashed forward, trapped it with his right foot and flicked it past Ricky Baker, who was storming up towards him. The good thing about playing your own team, Scott thought as he left Ricky standing, was that you knew everyone's weak spots.

"Square ball!" Ruby screamed again.

This time, Scott's pass was a gem. The ball flew through the air in a wide arc and landed at Ruby's feet. Wesley raced towards her, but Ruby was too quick for him. She tapped it past him and ran on towards the goal.

Only Danny stood between her and that all-important equaliser.

"Go on, Ruby!" Scott shouted.

And she did. As Danny raced out of the goal towards her, she booted the ball to his left.

Danny jumped up. He just got a hand to the ball. But it didn't change anything. As he fell to the muddy grass, the crowd gave a roar. Ruby had scored!

It was 1–1.

The girls' team crowded around their captain. They patted her on the back and told her what a fantastic goal she'd scored. Then, as Scott was making his way back up the pitch, Luke Edwards brushed against him on purpose.

"What are you up to?" he whispered. "Are you a boy – or a girlie?"

"Yeah, whose side are you on?" said someone else.

"Scumbag," hissed a third.

Scott turned – and was shocked by the way the boys were all looking at him.

Even Jack. "What's going on, Scott?" he said. "It was thanks to you she scored."

Scott gulped. Making the decision to play well was one thing. But now he had to put up with his team-mates bad-mouthing him.

"I ... I just want to win," he muttered.

"Typical," sneered Max Novak.

Scott felt anger rise inside him. "I've never played to lose," he shouted. "And I'm not going to start now."

Max snorted. "You never were a team player, were you, Scott?"

Scott's eyes blazed. "I'm not on your team now, am I?"

"Yeah, but—" Jack began.

Scott turned on him. "Have you forgotten what you told me?" he said. "It's the team that's important, not the individual player. Remember? And that's what I'm doing. Playing for the team."

"Well, I still think it stinks," said Max.

Scott smiled. "Do you know what, Max?" he said. "I don't give a monkey's bum what you think!"

Chapter 6

The score was still 1–1 at half-time. Mr Berryman and Mrs Hopkins came on to the pitch with trays of cut-up oranges. Without thinking, Scott made his way over to the boys.

Most of them turned their back on him. Max muttered something. Jack and Danny couldn't look their friend in the eye.

Pathetic, Scott thought as he headed back to the girls.

Sarah was there to greet him. "Fantastic pass," she said.

"Yeah, magic," said Ruby. "I'll have a few more like that in the second half, please."

"Same here," said Rosie Gartside.

"That's all very well," Scott laughed. "But I wouldn't mind scoring as well."

Ruby looked at him closely. "Are you sure?" she asked him. "Against Danny?"

Scott shrugged. If the boys were going to be mad with him, he'd make sure he gave them something to be mad about!

"Danny's the opposition," he said simply.

*

The second half started fast and furious. All twenty-two players were out there to win.

In the fifty-sixth minute, Luke Edwards came close to scoring for the boys. Then, ten minutes later, it was Scott's turn. An excellent cross from Ruby left him with the chance of a shot at goal.

He dashed forward. Ricky ran towards him – legs all over the place, not sure which way Scott was going. Scott flicked it this way, that way. The ball looked as if it was glued to the end of his boot. Then he tapped it between Ricky's legs.

Luke groaned. "Nutmegged."

Wesley saw what had happened. He dashed towards Scott to take over where Ricky had left off.

But Scott was ready for him. Not only had he seen Wesley running up, but he'd also spotted Rosie on his left. Drawing Wesley closer, he waited for the last possible moment before back-kicking the ball.

Rosie took control of the pass. She dribbled the ball to the right, nudged it forward and booted it with her left foot.

The shot wasn't that fast, but it was clever. It curved towards the post to Danny's left, spinning and dipping all the time. Danny grabbed at the ball. But it was no good. It grazed his fingers and spun into the far corner of the net.

For a moment, there was silence. The girls in the crowd could hardly believe their luck. Then, as the goal was given, a great roar went up, drowning out the boys' boos and whistles.

"Nice one, Scott," said Luke.

"Yeah, not bad – for a bunch of *girls*," Max hissed.

Even Jack turned away, muttering to himself.

Scott scowled but made no reply.

*

As the game started once more, everyone could see that the boys were in trouble. And not just because of Scott. At 2–1 now, the girls' team sensed victory. They raised their game. The backs defended superbly, closing down every attack. The midfield players ran rings around the opposition. Meanwhile, the forwards – Ruby, Rosie and Scott – were looking very dangerous.

"Come on!" Luke bellowed. "Let's get our act together."

Scott smiled. "They're rattled," he whispered as he jogged back past Ruby.

But then, in the seventy-first minute – and against the run of play –

the boys got their second goal. Jack had scored off a long pass from Luke.

It was 2–2. And with everything to play for.

The match got faster. The girls attacked the boys' goal again and again. The boys defended wildly, with foul after foul – lots of them aimed at Scott himself. And as the boys' game got dirtier, so the girls' team won more and more free kicks.

Then, with only twelve minutes of play left, Max got a hand-ball just outside the penalty box. The ref blew his whistle and gave another free kick to the girls. Sarah took it quickly. She tapped the ball to Rosie, who flicked it behind her. Sarah took back control of the ball, then kicked it high and wide to Ruby, out on the right wing.

"Perfect," Scott said to himself as he headed for the far post, taking care to keep Wesley between himself and the goal.

As Ruby dribbled the ball towards the goal, past Ricky, he grabbed her shirt. The linesman's flag went up. Ruby kicked the ball towards the goal. The flag remained up, but the referee had chosen to play the advantage.

"Good decision, ref," Scott said to himself as the ball came closer.

Out of the corner of his eye, he saw Danny race across the goal. The ball came closer still.

"Timing," said Scott. "It's all in the ... NOW!"

He jumped high into the air to meet the incoming ball and nodded it sharply down. Past Danny's flapping hands it went, over the line and into the back of the net.

Scott fell to his knees and threw back his head. "Yeah!" he roared. "YEAH!"

A cheer went up. Loud voices. Crazy, happy voices. *Girls'* voices chanting, "3–2! 3–2!"

As he headed back to the other end of the pitch, Scott understood what he'd done. Not only had he been playing well, but now he'd actually scored. Because of him, his team was ahead.

"But it's not over yet," he muttered grimly.

"You bet your life it isn't," said Max Novak, who had heard him. "Traitor," he added, and spat on the grass.

Scott flinched. *Traitor*. The word struck him like a punch on the jaw.

It was what he'd called Liam Griggs. And why? Because Griggs had scored against his old team. Now Scott had done exactly the same thing. He looked round at the other boys. Was that how they saw him – the same way he saw his ex-hero?

A traitor.

Chapter 7

With only five minutes left to play, it was looking as if the girls' team was going to win.

The boys were playing scrappily. They were behind, and it seemed as if they'd given up.

"Just keep your heads," Ruby told the rest of her team. "And nothing silly before that final whistle."

But then, when Rosie suddenly found herself with the ball – and unmarked – she decided to have a go at goal herself. She raced up the right wing, past Max, then Wesley, and was about to take a shot when Luke swooped in on her. He stole the ball from her and sped back in the opposite direction.

After a forty-metre run, and with nothing to lose, he decided to have a shot. He slammed the ball at the goal. It spun low and fast but shouldn't have been a problem for Tanya – but then it clipped Anna Parkin's heel.

Tanya threw herself at the ball – but she wasn't fast enough. And as she crashed to the ground, the deflected ball skidded under her body and into the net.

Every boy in the crowd roared. Things were looking good. At last. Their team had scored again.

3–3.

The girls' team lined up quickly and kicked off. Ruby kicked the ball to Rosie, who passed it to Sarah, who returned it to Ruby – all the while edging forward. Suddenly, Scott found himself in space. He shouted for the ball and, as Ruby kicked it forward, he started to run.

"Get him!" Max Novak howled.

Scott trapped the ball like a pro and ran with it up the pitch. Ruby went with him. Scott didn't care who he was playing with now. All he knew was that he wanted his team to win. And time was running out.

It was now or never.

As Wesley came speeding towards him, Scott looked across at Ruby. She nodded. He kicked the ball hard towards her. She put out her foot and the ball bounced back to where Scott – who had sped past Wesley – was waiting to collect it. A perfect one-two. The shouts from the crowd grew louder and louder.

"GIRLS!"

"BOYS!"

"GIRLS!"

"BOYS!"

On the pitch, the girls were moving up to support Scott. The boys were all over the place. Scott pressed on. The goal came closer. He clenched his teeth. He could do it.

He *would* do it!

Into the penalty area, Scott ran. He tapped the ball on to his left foot and ...

"*AARGH!*" he screamed as Ricky Baker's studded boot slammed into his left shin. It was agony. Scott crashed to the ground.

A blast of the whistle stopped the game. It was a penalty.

The referee dashed across to where Scott was lying, clutching his leg and moaning. He waved the first-aid team – Mr Berryman and

Mrs Hopkins – on to the pitch. They came trotting across the field with a bucket and a sponge.

Mr Berryman crouched down and felt around the wound. "Nasty," he said, "but it's not broken." He turned on Ricky. "That was shocking play!"

The referee thought the same. He put his hand in his back pocket, pulled out the red card and held it up to Ricky.

"Off," he snapped. "Now."

Danny had seen the foul clearer than anyone else. He came running over to his friend.

"Are you all right, mate?" he asked as Mrs Hopkins helped Scott to his feet.

Scott nodded as he put his weight down on his leg.

"Ouch!" he yelped. He took a few steps. "Yes ... Yes, it's OK. Just about."

The referee picked up the ball. "So who's going to take the penalty?" he asked.

"I will," said Ruby.

"No, I will."

Everyone turned and stared at Scott.

"You?" said Ruby. "But your leg ..."

"It's all right," said Scott.

"But this penalty's going to
decide the match," Ruby persisted.
"It's too important to—"

"He fouled *me*," said Scott. "It's *my* penalty.
I have the right to take it."

Ruby stared back. She could over-rule him.
After all, *she* was the captain of the team, not
Scott. Then again, if she had been fouled ...

"All right," she said at last. "But don't miss!"

Chapter 8

Scott hadn't even thought of missing. But as he placed the ball on the spot and got ready to take the penalty, he wondered if that might be the way to go.

No goal, and the score will stay at 3–3. A draw, he thought, and frowned.

Both teams had played well. The crowd had seen an excellent game. Maybe a draw would be the best result. After all, the match was always meant to be a laugh.

And yet, Scott knew, it had become serious. Deadly serious.

As he stepped back from the ball, the crowd went very quiet. Scott looked up. Danny was staring at him.

Then again, thought Scott, *can I do it anyway? Danny might be on the other team, but he's still my mate ...*

A win or a draw? That was the question.

Scott took a deep breath. He ran forward. He booted the ball hard to the left.

Danny leaped to the right.

Scott had tricked Danny. But would it be a goal? Or would the ball miss?

The crowd stayed silent. Then a loud roar went up and scarves and hats filled the air – white scarves, white hats – because the ball *had* found the corner of the net. Of course it had! Scott Marley could never have given anything

less than 100 per cent to make sure that his team would win.

The girls in the crowd went crazy, screaming and shouting and jumping up and down. Moments later, when the final whistle blew, the result was a spectacular 4–3 win to the girls' team.

The girls had beaten the boys.

*

As he made his way across the field, Scott kept his head down. The boos, jeers and loud comments from the boys, both in the crowd and on the pitch, were awful – and the cheers of the girls only made him feel worse.

Scott had made his mind up during the match. He would play to win. And they had won. But now that the match was over, Scott had to live with the result.

As the whooping and whistling, screaming and shouting slowly got quieter, a *tap tap tap* thudded round the football ground. Scott looked up. It was Mrs Brown. She was on the stage, checking that the microphone was working.

"A wonderful match," she said.

The crowd cheered.

"And to present the trophy to the winning team," she went on, "is someone who needs no introduction ..."

The man beside her stood up and pushed his hair back.

Scott squinted towards the stage. "It isn't," he muttered. "It can't be. I thought ..."

"Liam Griggs!" Mrs Brown announced.

Scott's heart missed a beat. It *was* him – the

man whose shirt he had chosen to wear, whose autograph he had begged and whose face had been on his wall for so long. Liam Griggs himself.

The traitor!

As he walked towards the stage with the others, Scott started to tremble. He'd have to shake hands with Griggs. That was what always happened when teams went up to collect a trophy. But how could he? How could he shake hands with the man who'd done the dirty on Albion?

He wouldn't. That was the answer. He'd pretend not to see Liam Griggs' hand and then he'd move on past him ...

At that moment, Liam Griggs – who was now holding the microphone – coughed and began to speak.

Chapter 9

"Ladies and gentlemen, girls and boys," Liam Griggs began. He looked around and smiled. "It is so good to be here."

Scott scowled.

"When Mrs Brown, your headteacher, first asked me," Griggs went on, "I wasn't sure. But when she explained *why* she wanted me to come, I changed my mind."

The crowd started to mutter. Like Scott, many of the boys and girls there felt that Liam Griggs had let them down – that he was a traitor.

"The hospital project means a lot to me," he said. "When I was four years old, I had my tonsils taken out. When I was eleven, I broke my leg. Both times, I ended up in the old children's ward. I understand why we need a new one."

Some of the crowd clapped. Most stayed silent.

"But there was another reason I came today ..."

Scott looked up. He saw Liam Griggs turn to Mrs Brown. The man looked worried. Unhappy. What was the matter with him?

Liam Griggs turned back. Then he took a deep breath. "Some of you here must be disappointed that I left Albion."

Several people in the crowd jeered.

"More than *disappointed*," Scott grumbled.

"To those fans who supported me from my first game for Albion ..." His voice cracked. "I ... I want to tell you why I left."

A hush fell.

"When I was a boy, I could see into the Albion football ground from my bedroom window," he said. "And from the moment I could kick a ball, I wanted to play for the team. Football was my life. I played at school. I played in a local club. Then one day, a scout for Albion saw me play and invited me to a training session. Can you imagine how I felt?"

Scott nodded. It was the moment that *he* had dreamed about for so long.

"Then I signed the contract. I was on the team. My dream had come true!"

Scott smiled.

"I had the time of my life at Albion," Griggs went on. "It was my home, and I wouldn't change a thing ..."

"So why did you go?" an angry voice shouted out from the crowd.

"Trust me," said Liam Griggs, "I know how you feel. I felt just like you when Tom Grant – Tom Grant, my childhood hero – upped and went to City. I thought he was a traitor." He shook his head. "But I was wrong."

Scott frowned. "Why?" he shouted, and the word boomed all around the football ground.

"Yeah, why?" others shouted. "*Why?*"

Liam Griggs turned to Scott. "I'll tell you why. Home is a wonderful place. It prepares you for everything that lies ahead. But sooner or later, it's time to move on. To leave home. And when that time comes, only a fool would ignore it."

Scott looked away. Whatever Griggs said, he had left his team-mates – and then, at the first chance, had scored against them.

"Other teams tried to sign me up before," Griggs went on. "Lots of teams. I always said no." He frowned. "But when United offered me a place, I knew it was time to move on." He smiled. "Time to leave home."

Scott scratched his head. Perhaps Griggs was right. Albion was big – but United was much bigger. They might even win the Europa League this year ...

Suddenly, Scott could see that he'd been unfair to Liam Griggs. Yes, Griggs had scored against his old team. But so had Scott. That very afternoon. And not once, but twice!

"So that was what I did," Griggs said. "I moved on. I left home."

For a moment, the crowd stayed silent. Would they understand and clap? Or would they start booing?

Scott looked around. He felt bad. Liam Griggs had come to the match to tell his story to his old home-town crowd ...

Without even thinking, Scott started to clap. Others joined in. Then someone cheered. Then someone else. The next moment, *everyone* in the football ground was clapping and cheering!

"Thank you," said Liam Griggs with a happy smile. "Thank you all."

He picked up the silver cup.

"That was an amazing match!" he said. "Bad luck to the losers. And well done to the winners. Would the girls' team please step up to receive the Charity Cup."

He lifted the trophy high.

"It was a fantastic game of skill and spirit and, most important of all, teamwork!"

Mrs Brown smiled. This was more like it. And, as Ruby, Scott and the rest of the team went up onto the stage, Liam Griggs went on.

"It was teamwork that got the hospital charity set up," he said. "Teamwork that made the match possible. And teamwork that gave us all such a great display of football."

Scott moved along the front of the stage towards Liam Griggs. He felt his heart *thump – thump – thump* in his chest. He saw now that not shaking hands with the man was stupid. Childish.

Finally, it was his turn. He held out his hand – but could not look up.

"Excellent game," Liam Griggs said, and gripped Scott's hand. "Scott, isn't it?"

Scott couldn't speak. Liam Griggs – his hero – was shaking his hand *and* congratulating him! His head spun. His legs felt weak.

"Scott Marley," he said at last.

Griggs let go of his hand. "And you support Albion, yeah?"

Scott nodded. He felt embarrassed for shouting out the way he had. "You ... you autographed my ticket once," he said, and looked up. "I used to wear your shirt."

"But not any more," said Griggs with a little smile.

Scott shrugged. "I'm not a United fan," he said simply.

Griggs leaned forward. "Neither am I," he said softly. "I'll always be an Albion fan."

"But you scored against us last week," said Scott hotly.

"Because I play for United now," said Griggs. "The team has to come first." He smiled. "There's no 'I' in 'team', is there? After this afternoon's game, Scott, I thought you understood that better than anyone!"

Scott sighed. "You mean, playing on the girls' team?" he said. "I had to. They were one player short and—"

"I know everything that happened," Griggs broke in. "And you did the right thing. A lot of lads would have tried to throw the game, to keep in with their mates. But not you. You gave your all to the team you were playing for. And I really admire that. You should be well proud of yourself."

Scott looked down. He felt embarrassed by all the praise he was getting – though a part of him also hoped that Max Novak, Luke Edwards and all the others were listening.

Chapter 10

It was the end of the afternoon, the winning team had collected the cup and the stands began to empty. The two Year 7 football teams headed for the changing room in twos and threes – apart from one person, who stood by himself at the back.

Scott Marley.

He'd come back down to earth with a bump. The match was over. Scott had helped the girls win, but he didn't feel a part of their team any more. As for the boys – they wanted nothing to do with him.

Of course, Scott wasn't surprised that Luke and Max were ignoring him. But it hurt him that Danny and Jack were doing the same.

They'll come round sooner or later, Scott told himself. He sighed. *Sooner, I hope.*

Oddly, it wasn't Danny or Jack who spoke to Scott first – but Max Novak. Halfway across the pitch, he stopped, turned and put out his hand.

"No hard feelings," he said.

Scott looked back at Max for a moment. The other boys watched the two of them. Then Scott went to shake hands. As he did so, Max snatched his hand away and scratched the back of his head, a mocking smile on his face.

"Sucker," he hissed.

The others laughed. Scott's face turned red.

"What's it feel like – being a traitor?" Max asked.

Ignore him, Scott told himself.

"And what a nice chat you had with Liam Griggs," Max went on. "Another traitor!"

The others laughed again. All of them – except for Danny and Jack, but even they didn't help their friend. Max smiled.

"I said, another trait—"

"I heard what you said!" Scott exploded. He spun round. "What would *you* have done?"

"Me?" said Max. He smirked at the others. "I'd have made sure the boys won."

"Yeah?" said Scott.

"Yeah," said Max.

"That's cos you're an idiot," said Scott. "A player has to be loyal to the team ..."

"Is that what Traitor Griggs told you?" said Max with a sneer.

"Don't be stupid, Max," Jack butted in. "Scott decided what to do before he knew Griggs was there."

At last, thought Scott. *Someone standing up for me.*

Max turned on Jack. "Keep out of it," he said. "This is between me and Scott – our so-called captain, who'd rather see the other side win."

The words filled Scott's head. Max had been at it all afternoon. Sneering. Jeering. Making nasty little comments. So far, Scott had kept his temper. But enough was enough!

"That's it," he roared. He shoved Max hard in the chest.

Max fell back. Then, head down, he threw himself at Scott. They both crashed to the ground.

"Take that back," Scott snarled as he pinned Max down.

"No way!" Max screamed. He brought his knee up hard into Scott's stomach.

Scott groaned and fell to the side. Max was on him at once. They rolled over. Kicking. Punching. Max was big, but Scott's anger was making him stronger.

"Take it back!" he shouted, and his fist slammed into Max's jaw. "Take it back or ..."

Suddenly, two hands were at the back of Scott's shirt. He was pulled away.

"Stop! This!" someone roared. *"Now!"*

Scott spun round. Mr Berryman was glaring at him. "Scott, I'm surprised at you," he said.

Scott hung his head.

"As for you!" Mr Berryman shouted at Max. "Get showered, lad. Go on, get out of my sight."

Max turned and headed for the changing rooms.

"And the rest of you," said Mr Berryman, looking round. "Does anyone else want to have a go at Scott for how he played this afternoon?"

The boys looked down at the ground.

"Well?" said Mr Berryman.

"No," someone muttered. The others shook their heads.

"Good," he said. "Scott did the right thing. He gave everything for his team. And that's the type of player we – *you* – need as captain. So, no more talk of *traitors*. All right?"

The boys nodded.

"OK, then," said Mr Berryman. "Go and get changed."

The boys turned and headed off. Scott went with them. At first, he was on his own. But Mr Berryman was glad to see others soon join him. They slapped him on the back. They told him there were no hard feelings – and they meant it.

Mr Berryman smiled. "All's well that ends well," he said softly.

*

Later that evening, Scott, Danny and Jack met up – as ever – at the rec. Not that any of them felt that much like playing. After all there was far too much to talk about. The match. The fight ...

"It's certainly been an action-packed day," said Scott.

"You can say that again," said Jack.

"It's certainly been an action-packed day."

"Idiot," said Jack, and laughed.

"So what did he say to you?" Danny asked.

"Who?" said Scott.

"Who?" said Danny, and punched him on the arm. "The great Liam Griggs, of course."

Scott smiled. "Loads of things. Didn't you hear?"

Jack and Danny shook their heads.

"We were too far back," said Jack.

Scott shrugged. He didn't want to tell them what Liam Griggs said about him playing really well. "He ... He said he's still an Albion supporter," Scott said after a bit.

"And you believe that?" said Danny.

"Yes," said Scott. He nodded. "Yes, I do now.
He's playing for his team. He's not a traitor.
And neither am I," he added. "For him, for me,
for all of us – that's what it's all about ..."

"TEAMWORK!" the three of them yelled.

Our books are tested
for children and young people by
children and young people.

Thanks to everyone who consulted on
a manuscript for their time and effort in
helping us to make our books better
for our readers.